WOL PIN

Alfred A. Knopf
Random House/Singer School Division
First Voices The second book
edited by Geoffrey Summerfield

First Voices The second book

edited by Geoffrey Summerfield

ALFRED A. KNOPF
Alfred A. Knopf, Inc.
New York

RANDOM HOUSE/SINGER SCHOOL DIVISION
Random House, Inc.
New York • Brandon, Miss. • Dallas • Atlanta • Los Altos

Contents

Riddles

It is in the rock, but not in the stone;
It is in the marrow, but not in the bone;
It is in the bolster, but not in the bed;
It is not in the living, nor yet in the dead.

The land was white,
   The seed was black;
It'll take a good scholar
   To riddle me that.

On yonder hill there is a red deer,
The more you shoot it, the more you may
You cannot drive that deer away.

As I went over London Bridge
Upon a cloudy day
I met a fellow clothed in yellow.
I took him up and sucked his blood,
And threw his skin away.

In marble halls as white as milk,
Lined with a skin as soft as silk,
Within a fountain crystal-clear,
A golden apple doth appear.
No doors there are to this stronghold,
Yet thieves break in and steal the gold.

TRADITIONAL ENGLISH

Who Said?

'There's-not-a cobbler-in-the-world-
Can-make-a shoe-to-me-
To-me-to-me-to-me-
Why-so-why-so-why-so-why-so?-
Because-my-heel's-as-long-as-my-toe-
My-toe-my-toe-my-toe!'

ANONYMOUS

The Little Man with Wooden Hair

There was a little man with wooden hair
Who'd sneak into the rear of buses
And holler, 'Somebody just ate my mother!'
For that way, of course, he could count on a quick trim
Without having to pay for the broken window.

KENNETH PATCHEN

A Conversation

ROSIE PROBERT What seas did you see,
Tom Cat, Tom Cat,
In your sailoring days
Long long ago?
What sea beasts were
In the wavery green
When you were my master?

CAPTAIN CAT I'll tell you the truth.
Seas barking like seals,
Blue seas and green,
Seas covered with eels
And mermen and whales.

ROSIE What seas did you sail
Old whaler when
On the blubbery waves
Between Frisco and Wales
officer of the deck You were my bosun?

CAPTAIN CAT As true as I'm here
You landlubber Rosie
You cozy love
My easy as easy
My true sweetheart,
Seas green as a bean
Seas gliding with swans
In the seal-barking moon.

DYLAN THOMAS

The Mouse that Gnawed the Oak-Tree Down

The mouse that gnawed the oak-tree down
Began his task in early life.
He kept so busy with his teeth
He had no time to take a wife.

He gnawed and gnawed through sun and rain
When the ambitious fit was on,
Then rested in the sawdust till
A month of idleness had gone.

groups

He did not move about to hunt
The coteries of mousie-men.
He was a snail-paced, stupid thing
Until he cared to gnaw again.

The mouse that gnawed the oak-tree down,
When that tough foe was at his feet –
Found in the stump no angel-cake
Nor buttered bread, nor cheese nor meat –

The forest-roof let in the sky.
'This light is worth the work,' said he.
'I'll make this ancient swamp more light,'
And started on another tree.

VACHEL LINDSAY

To Be Closely Written on a Small Piece of Paper Which Folded into a Tight Lozenge Will Fit Any Girl's Locket

Lo the leaves
Upon the new autumn grass –
Look at them well. !

WILLIAM CARLOS WILLIAMS

The Tramp Tree

hanging The tree with braces angin out
Like rags of a Tramp.
When the tree sways in the wind
Its like a tramps arm with hairs on.
Their fingers at the top of the tree,
Their tearing fingers,
Tearing holes in the sky,
Trying to grab what isn't there
Trying to get free.
Spiky grass is his hair
And half his head is under the grass
With his brain as dirt
The roots are like veins
Pulled out with the strength of his arms
His body with worms all wriggling about
Keeping him down
The stones that he eats
Fall down his throat
And stop at an end.

ANTHONY BARTON Age 9

One Bright Morning

One bright morning in the middle of the night,
Two dumb boys got up to fight.
Back to back they faced each other,
Drew their swords and shot each other.
A deaf policeman heard the noise,
Came and arrested those two dumb boys.

TRADITIONAL AMERICAN

Dream Song

Daybreak people have been chirping.
Above on the roof
Alighting they chirp.

TRADITIONAL
North American Indian poem translated from the Wintun by D. Demetracopoulou

The Cloud-Mobile

Above my face is a map
where continents form and fade.
Blue countries, made
on a white sea, are erased;
white countries are traced
on a blue sea.

It is a map that moves
faster than real
but so slow;
only my watching proves
that island has being,
or that bay.

It is a model of time;
mountains are wearing away,
coasts cracking, the ocean
spills over, then new
hills heap into view
with river-cuts of blue between them.

It is a map of change:
this is the way things are
with a stone or a star.
This is the way things go,
hard or soft,
swift or slow.

MAY SWENSON

In a Sailplane

Still as a bird
Transfixed in flight
We shiver and flow
Into leagues of light.

Rising and turning
Without a sound
As summer lifts us
Off the ground.

The sky's deep bell
Of glass rings down.
We slip in a sea
That cannot drown.

We kick the wide
Horizon's blues
Like a cluttering hoop
From round our shoes.

This easy plane
So quietly speaks,
Like a tree it sighs
In silvery shrieks.

Neatly we soar
Through a roaring cloud:
Its caverns of snow
Are dark and loud.

Into banks of sun
Above the drifts
Of quilted cloud
Our stillness shifts.

Here no curious
Bird comes near.
We float alone
In a snowman's sphere.

Higher than spires
Where breath is rare
We beat the shires
Of racing air.

Up the cliff
Of sheer no-place
We swarm a rope
That swings on space.

Breezed by a star's
Long-drawn-out Protracted stare
We watch the earth
Drop out of air.

Red stars of light
Burn on the round
Of land: street-constellations
Strew the ground.

Their bridges leap
From town to town:
Into lighted dusk
We circle down.

Still as a bird
Transfixed in flight
We come to nest
In the field of night.

JAMES KIRKUP

Sitting Down, Looking Up

A silver jet,
riding the top of tundra clouds,
comes over
maybe from Rio:
the aluminium sun shines
on it
as if it were a natural creature.

A. R. AMMONS

Song: The Railway Train

You see the smoke at Kapunda
The steam puffs regularly,
Showing quickly, it looks like frost,
It runs like running water,
It blows like a spouting whale.

TRADITIONAL Australian Aboriginal poem translated by George Taplin

Between Walls

the back wings
of the

hospital where
nothing

will grow lie
cinders

in which shine
the broken

pieces of a green
bottle

WILLIAM CARLOS WILLIAMS

16 een bumfrey

Roads

Twisting turning
clinging to the contours of the earth
black – black as night
with white lines down its back.

MEI-LAN LAW Age 11

Borrowed Armor

Borrowed armor, old,
   getting fitted to my body –
      oh, it's cold!

BUSON Japanese poem translated by Harold G. Henderson

The World Upside Down

A trout leaps high –
   below him, in the river bottom,
      clouds flow by.

ONITSURA Japanese poem translated by Harold G. Henderson

Sudden Shower

Not even a hat –
   and cold rain falling on me?
      Tut-tut! think of that!

BASHŌ Japanese poem translated by Harold G. Henderson

18 tother bumfrey

Didn't It Rain

Now, didn't it rain, chillun,
God's gonna 'stroy this world with water,
Now didn't it rain, my Lord,
Now didn't it rain, rain, rain.

Well, it rained forty days and it rained forty nights,
There wasn't no land nowhere in sight,
God sent a raven to carry the news,
lifted, hoisted He histe his wings and away he flew.

Well, it rained forty days and forty nights without
    stopping,
Noah was glad when the rain stopped a-dropping.
God sent Noah a rainbow sign,
Says, 'No more water, but fire next time.'

They knocked at the window and they knocked at the
    door,
They cried, 'O Noah, please take me on board.'
Noah cried, 'You're full of sin,
The Lord's got the key and you can't get in.'

TRADITIONAL AMERICAN

It ain't gonna rain no more, no more

It ain't gonna rain no more, no more,
It ain't gonna rain no more;
How in the heck can I wash my neck
If it ain't gonna rain no more?

TRADITIONAL AMERICAN

Praise Song of the Wind

Trees with weak roots
I will strike, I the wind.
I will roar, I will whistle.

small piles of hay   Haycocks built today
I will scatter, I the wind.
I will roar, I will whistle.

Badly made haycocks
I will carry off, I the wind.
I will roar, I will whistle.

Uncovered stacks of sheaves
I will soak through, I the wind.
I will roar, I will whistle.

Houses not tightly roofed
I will destroy, I the wind.
I will roar, I will whistle.

Hay piled in sheds
I will tear apart, I the wind.
I will roar, I will whistle.

Fire kindled in the road
I will set flickering, I the wind.
I will roar, I will whistle.

Houses with bad smoke-holes
I will shake, I the wind.
I will roar, I will whistle.

The farmer who does not think
I will make to think, I the wind.
I will roar, I will whistle.

The worthless slug-a-bed
I will wake, I the wind.
I will roar, I will whistle.

TRADITIONAL Siberian poem translated by W. Radloff and Willard R. Trask

Storm Tide on Mejit

The wind's spine is broken,
It blows less,
We perform the wind-taboo.
It grows still, still, still,
Wholly still,
The calm, the calm.
The wind-taboo, *e*,
Makes calm, calm, calm.
The surf, surf, surf,
The surf, surf, surf,
The surf, surf, surf,
Plunges, roars,
Plunges, roars,
Plunges, roars,
It flows up,
The sea covers the beach with foam,
It is full of the finest sand,
Stirring up the ground, stirring up the ground.
It slaps, slaps, slaps,
Slaps, slaps, slaps
On the beach, and roars.

TRADITIONAL
Marshall Islands poem translated from a Micronesian language
by Augustin Krämer and Willard R. Trask

Over the dark highway

Over the dark highway
over the woods
and the clusters of small houses,
the clouds appear

The great clouds of a winter twilight!

> When I see them I feel like a hundred men
> who know they have slipped out of prison
> without a trace

LOU LIPSITZ

The Computer's Spring Greeting

Spring gling
flingle jingle
jing wring
sing wing
bring ting
ring ding
dingle ding
ding a ling
ling a ring
ring ring
jing a ring
wing a ling
spring a ling
spring swing
wing ing
fling spring
sprang spring
SPR . . . . . . ING!
   SPRING

GARY LEWIS Age 9

Summer Night

A lightning flash:
   between the forest trees
     I have seen water.

SHIKI Japanese poem translated by Harold G. Henderson

Dull Day

The day was dull,
The smell of the air
was icy.

The color of the air
was as Dark
as a wolf's coat,
Misty.

DAVID HILL Age 8

The Cat and the Moon

The cat went here and there
And the moon spun round like a top,
And the nearest kin of the moon,
The creeping cat, looked up.
Black Minnaloushe stared at the moon,
For, wander and wail as he would,
The pure cold light in the sky
Troubled his animal blood.
Minnaloushe runs in the grass
Lifting his delicate feet.
Do you dance, Minnaloushe, do you dance?
When two close kindred meet,
What better than call a dance?
Maybe the moon may learn,
Tired of that courtly fashion,
A new dance turn.
Minnaloushe creeps through the grass
From moonlit place to place,
The sacred moon overhead
Has taken a new phase.
Does Minnaloushe know that his pupils
Will pass from change to change,
And that from round to crescent,
From crescent to round they range?
Minnaloushe creeps through the grass
Alone, important and wise,
And lifts to the changing moon
His changing eyes.

W. B. YEATS

Tree-Disease

On the moon with great ease
You can catch tree-disease.
The symptoms are birds
Seeming interested in your words
And examining your ears.
Then a root peers
From under the nail
Of your big toe, then
You'd better get cured quick
Or you'll be really sick.

TED HUGHES

Which?

'What did you say?'
'I? Nothing.' 'No?...
What was that sound?'
'When?'
'Then.'
'I do not know.'
'Whose eyes were those on us?'
'Where?'
'There.'
'No eyes I saw.'
'Speech, footfall, presence – how cold the night may be!'
'Phantom or fantasy, it's all one to *me*.'

WALTER DE LA MARE

Slieve Gua

Gua Mountain

Slieve Gua, craggy and black wolf-den:
In the clefts the wind howls,
In its dens the wolves wail.

bellows

Autumn on Slieve Gua and the angry
Brown deer bells, and herons
Croak across Slieve Gua's crags.

TRADITIONAL IRISH

I am John Jones

'I am John Jones.'
'Take a chair.'
'Yes, and I am the son of John
 Throckmorton Jones.'
'Is that possible? Take two chairs.'

CARL SANDBURG

Social Studies

Woody says, 'Let's *make* our soap.
It's easy.
We learned about it
In school.'
He told Mother,
'All you do is
Take a barrel.
Bore holes in the sides,
And fill it with straw.
Ashes on top –'

'No,' said Mother.

MARY NEVILLE

Nora

I was not sleeping when Brother said
'Good-bye!' and laughed and teased my head;
And went, like rockets, out of the door,
As he had done most days before.

But it was fun to curl between
The white warm sheets, and not be seen,

And stay, a minute more, alone,
Keeping myself for my very own.

GWENDOLYN BROOKS

Poem

I can hear the trees whispering
The cat purring
The dogs barking
no wonder I cant get to sleep
I can hear my dad in a rage
tearing up a page
into little bits
while my mother sits
crying
no wonder I cant get to sleep

SUSAN DAVID Age 8

Gravel Paths

I feel crinkled when I walk on gravel paths.
The gravel crinkles me
And I become gravel,
Crunched under five thousand footsteps.
I know what it is to be gravel,
Pecked at by pigeons,
Searching for crumbs of park picnics.

Gravel gets tired,
Being poked at by sparrows and pigeons,
Being squashed under grown-up feet,
Being combed by park men's tickling rakes.
Gravel would rather play,
Explode in skittery sprays under running sneakers.
At least I think it would,
And I should know,
Having run crinkled
And sneaker-shod
Up many gravel paths.

PATRICIA HUBBELL

Angry

You feel as if you could jump on them,
As if to kill them in anger,
It feels as if you had the strength,
Of a hundred men.
You get in a kind of a trance,
And go pushing people about,
The slightest thing that goes wrong,
Makes you blame it on someone else
If a person gets angry with you,
You try not to listen.

JOHN DONALD WILLIAMS Age 11

What's the matter up there?

'What's the matter up there?'
'Playing soldiers.'
'But soldiers don't make that kind of noise.'
'We're playing the kind of soldier that
makes that kind of noise.'

CARL SANDBURG

The Big Rock Candy Mountains

On a summer's day in the month of May,
A burly bum come a-hiking,
Traveling down that lonesome road
A-looking for his liking.
He was headed for a land that was far away,
Beside them crystal fountains –
'I'll see you all this coming fall
In the Big Rock Candy Mountains.'

In the Big Rock Candy Mountains
You never change your socks,
And little streams of alcohol
Come a-trickling down the rocks.
The box cars are all empty
policemen And the railroad bulls are blind,
There's a lake of stew and whisky, too,
You can paddle all around 'em in a big canoe
In the Big Rock Candy Mountains.

 O – the buzzing of the bees in the cigarette trees
 Round the soda-water fountains,
 Where the lemonade springs and the bluebird sings
 In the Big Rock Candy Mountains.

In the Big Rock Candy Mountains,
There's a land that's fair and bright,
Where the hand-outs grow on bushes
And you sleep out every night,
Where the box cars are all empty
And the sun shines every day,
O I'm bound to go, where there ain't no snow,
Where the rain don't fall and the wind don't blow
In the Big Rock Candy Mountains.

In the Big Rock Candy Mountains
The jails are made of tin
And you can bust right out again
As soon as they put you in;
The farmers' trees are full of fruit,
The barns are full of hay,
I'm going to stay where you sleep all day,
Where they boiled in oil the inventor of toil
In the Big Rock Candy Mountains.

TRADITIONAL AMERICAN

A Tragic Story

wise man   There liv'd a sage in days of yore,
And he a handsome pigtail wore,
But wonder'd much and sorrow'd more,
Because it hung behind him.

He mus'd upon this curious case,
And swore he'd change the pigtail's place,
And have it hanging at his face,
Not dangling there behind him.

Says he, 'The mystery I've found –
I'll turn me round.'
He turn'd him round,
But still it hung behind him.

Then round and round, and out and in,
All day the puzzled sage did spin;
In vain – it matter'd not a pin,
The pigtail hung behind him.

And right and left, and round about,
And up and down, and in and out
He turn'd, but still the pigtail stout
Hung steadily behind him.

And though his efforts never slack,
And though he twist, and twirl, and tack,
Alas! still faithful to his back,
The pigtail hangs behind him.

WILLIAM MAKEPEACE THACKERAY

The Signifying Monkey

The Monkey and the Lion
Got to talking one day.
Monkey looked down and said, 'Lion,
I hear you're king in every way.
But I know somebody
Who do not think that is true –
He told me he could whip
The living daylights out of you.'
Lion said, 'Who?'
Monkey said, 'Lion,
He talked about your mama
And talked about your grandma, too,
And I'm too polite to tell you
What he said about you.'
Lion said, 'Who said what? Who?'
Monkey in the tree,
Lion on the ground.
Monkey kept on signifying
But he didn't come down.
Monkey said, 'His name is Elephant –
He stone sure is not your friend.'
Lion said, 'He don't need to be
Because today will be his end.'

Lion took off through the jungle
Lickity-split,
Meaning to grab Elephant
And tear him bit to bit. Full stop!
He came across Elephant copping a righteous nod
Under a fine cool shady tree.
Lion said, 'You big old no-good so-and-so,
It's either you or me.'
Lion let out a solid roar
And bopped Elephant with his paw.
Elephant just took his trunk
And busted old Lion's jaw.
Lion let out another roar,
Reared up six feet tall.
Elephant just kicked him in the belly
And laughed to see him drop and fall.
Lion rolled over,
Copped Elephant by the throat.
Elephant just shook him loose
And butted him like a goat,
Then he tromped him and he stomped him
Till the Lion yelled, 'Oh, no!'
And it was near-nigh sunset
When Elephant let Lion go.
The signifying Monkey
Was still sitting in his tree
When he looked down and saw the Lion.
Said, 'Why, Lion, who can that there be?'
Lion said, 'Monkey, I don't want
To hear your jive-end jive.'
Monkey just kept on signifying,
'Lion, you for sure caught hell –
Mister Elephant's whipped you
To a fare-thee-well!
You ain't no king to me.
Fact is, I don't think that you
Can even as much as roar –
And if you try I'm liable

To come down out of this tree and
Whip your tail some more.'
The Monkey started laughing
And jumping up and down.
But he jumped so hard the limb broke
And he landed – bam! – on the ground.
When he went to run, his foot slipped
And he fell flat down.
Grrr-rrr-rr-r! The Lion was on him
With his front feet and his hind.
Monkey hollered, 'Ow!
I didn't mean it, Mister Lion!'
Lion said, 'You little flea-bag you!
Why, I'll eat you up alive.
I wouldn't a-been in this fix a-tall
Wasn't for your signifying jive.'
'*Please*,' said Monkey, 'Mister Lion,
If you'll just let me go,
I got something to tell you, please,
I think you ought to know.'
Lion let the Monkey loose
To see what his tale could be –
And Monkey jumped right back on up
Into his tree.
'What I was gonna tell you,' said Monkey,
'Is you square old so-and-so,
If you fool with me I'll get
Elephant to whip your head some more.'
'Monkey,' said the Lion,
Beat to his unbooted knees,
'You and all your signifying children
Better stay up in them trees.'
Which is why today
Monkey does his signifying
A-way-up out of the way.

TRADITIONAL AMERICAN

Ooh!

Now, miller, miller, dustipole,
I'll clapper-claw your jobbernole!

TRADITIONAL ENGLISH

Day of Rabblement

O come here! a sunflower!
No no no no
O hurry! hurry!
A sunflower is standing here!

No no no no

O come here!
There's a sunflower beside the wall!
No no no no
Great God! hurry! a sunflower!

No no no no

A sunflower!
Come! look at the sunflower!
Sunflower!
No no no no
Then tell me why you
Won't come!
No no no no

No no no no.

KENNETH PATCHEN

Mean Song

Snickles and podes,
Ribble and grodes:
That's what I wish you.

A nox in the groot,
A root in the stoot
And a gock in the forbeshaw, too.

Keep out of sight
For fear that I might
Glom you a gravely snave.

Don't show your face
Around any place
Or you'll get one flack snack in the bave.

EVE MERRIAM

The Feast of Lanterns

Tching-a-ring-a-ring-tching,
Feast of Lanterns,
What a lot of chop-sticks, bombs and gongs;
Four-and-twenty thousand crink-um-crank-ums,
All among the bells and the ding-dongs.

TRADITIONAL ENGLISH

We four lads from Liverpool are

We four lads from Liverpool are:
Paul in a taxi, John in a car,
George on a scooter, tootin' his hooter,
Following Ringo Starr!

TRADITIONAL ENGLISH

Rattlesnake

Rattlesnake, O rattlesnake,
What makes your teeth so white?
I've been in the bottom all my life,
An' I ain't done nothin' but bite, bite,
Ain't done nothin' but bite.

Muskrat, O muskrat,
What makes you smell so bad?
I've been in the bottom all of my life
Till I'm mortified in my head, head,
I'm mortified in my head.

Groundhog, groundhog,
What makes your back so brown?
It's a wonder I don't smotherfy,
Livin' down in the ground, ground,
Livin' down in the ground.

Rooster, O rooster,
What makes your claws so hard?
Been scratchin' this gravel all my days,
It's a wonder I ain't tired, tired,
It's a wonder I ain't tired.

Jaybird, O jaybird,
What makes you fly so high?
Been robbin' your cornpatch all my life,
It's a wonder I don't die, die,
It's a wonder I don't die.

TRADITIONAL AMERICAN

Riches

The ditch in Humber Lane
Was black with tadpoles, round
Black beads and whippy tails;
I knelt down at the side,
And filled my jar as black
As now I fill this page,
Glad of the gathered life
However many died.

ROBIN SKELTON,

On a Sunday

On a Sunday, when the place was closed,
I saw a plump mouse among the cakes in the window:
dear ladies,
who crowd this expensive tearoom,
you must not think that you alone are blessed of God.

CHARLES REZNIKOFF

The shopgirls leave their work

The shopgirls leave their work
quietly.

Machines are still, tables and chairs
darken.

The silent rounds of mice and roaches begin.

CHARLES REZNIKOFF

The cock again

The cock again
   is fighting like a lion:
      see his mane!

KIKAKU Japanese poem translated by Harold G. Henderson

The Open-Air Bath

There is no place
   to throw the used bath water.
      Insect cries!

ONITSURA Japanese poem translated by Harold G. Henderson

The Bee

The bee is a merchant.
He trades among
flower planets.

PETER KELSO Age 12

The Whale

A whale!
   Down it goes, and more and more
      up goes its tail!

BUSON Japanese poem translated by Harold G. Henderson

from Oliphaunt

Gray as a mouse,
Big as a house,
Nose like a snake,
I make the earth shake,
As I tramp through the grass;
Trees crack as I pass.
With horns in my mouth
I walk in the South,
Flapping big ears.
Beyond count of the years
I stump round and round,
Never lie on the ground,
Not even to die.
Oliphaunt am I,
Biggest of all,
Huge, old and tall.
If ever you'd met me,
You wouldn't forget me.
If ever you do,
You won't think I'm true;
But Old Oliphaunt am I,
And I never lie.

J. R. R. TOLKIEN

Beg Parding

'Beg parding, Mrs. Harding,
 Is my kitting in your garding?'
'Yes she is, and all alone,
 Chewing of a mutting bone.'

ANONYMOUS

Cat and the Weather

Cat takes a look at the weather.
Snow.
Puts a paw on the sill.
His perch is piled, is a pillow.

Shape of his pad appears.
Will it dig? No.
Not like sand.
Like his fur almost.

But licked, not liked.
Too cold.
Insects are flying, fainting down.
He'll try

to bat one against the pane.
They have no body and no buzz.
And now his feet are wet;
it's a puzzle.

Shakes each leg,
then shakes his skin
to get the white flies off.
Looks for his tail,

tells it to come on in
by the radiator.
World's turned queer
somehow. All white,

no smell. Well, here
inside it's still familiar.
He'll go to sleep until
it puts itself right.

MAY SWENSON

Duck

She waddles through the dust
In which no fish are smiling
Within her sides she carries
The restlessness of water

Clumsy
She waddles slowly
The reeds she's thinking of
She'll reach them anyway

Never
Never will she be able
To walk
As she was able
To plow the mirrors

VASKO POPA
Yugoslavian poem translated from the Serbo-Croatian by Anne Pennington

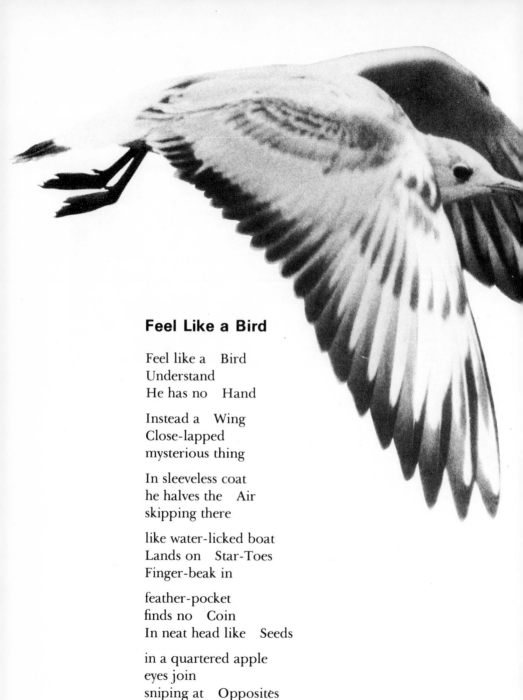

Feel Like a Bird

Feel like a   Bird
Understand
He has no   Hand

Instead a   Wing
Close-lapped
mysterious thing

In sleeveless coat
he halves the   Air
skipping there

like water-licked boat
Lands on   Star-Toes
Finger-beak in

feather-pocket
finds no   Coin
In neat head like   Seeds

in a quartered apple
eyes join
sniping at   Opposites

to stereoscope
the scene before
Close to floor   Giddy

no arms to fling
a third   Sail
spreads for calm

his tail
Hand better than a   Wing
to gather a   Heap

to count
to clasp a   Mate?
Or leap

lone-free on muffled
shoulders to span
a   Fate?

MAY SWENSON

The Rook

Black as night it cuts through the air,
Its wide wings spread,
Flap and wave.
Scavenger.
Soft of touch,
But as tough as leather.
Oily wings like cast-off rags,
The rook.
A ready beak to tear and rip,
Eyes like coals, cold and dark,
With hoarse cry
And stupid.

JAMES EARP Age 12

Eskimo Hunting Song

I wanted to use my weapon.
There was a big blubbery seal on the ice, even here.
I struck smartly with my harpoon,
And then I just pulled it up, the seal wandering from
    one breathing-hole to another.

I wanted to use my weapon.
There was a big antlered caribou on the land, even down
    there.
I shot my arrow swiftly,
Then I just knocked it down in this place, the caribou
    that wandered about the land.

I wanted to use my weapon.
There was a fish right in the lake, even here.
I struck it smartly with my fish-spear,
Then I just pulled it up, the fish that wandered about
    down here.

I wanted to use my weapon.
There was a big bearded seal, just at the river-mouth,
    even here.
I paddled my kayak hard,
Then I simply towed it ashore, just at the river-mouth.

TRADITIONAL Eskimo poem translated by Sir Maurice Bowra

The Ballad of Red Fox

Yellow sun yellow
Sun yellow sun,
When, oh, when
Will red fox run?

When the hollow horn shall sound,
When the hunter lifts his gun
And liberates the wicked hound,
Then, oh, then shall red fox run.

Yellow sun yellow
Sun yellow sun,
Where, oh, where
Will red fox run?

Through meadows hot as sulphur,
Through forests cool as clay,
Through hedges crisp as morning
And grasses limp as day.

Yellow sky yellow
Sky yellow sky,
How, oh, how
Will red fox die?

With a bullet in his belly,
A dagger in his eye,
And blood upon his red red brush
Shall red fox die.

MELVIN WALKER LA FOLLETTE

Living Tenderly

My body a rounded stone
with a pattern of smooth seams.
My head a short snake,
retractive, projective.
My legs come out of their sleeves
or shrink within,
and so does my chin.
My eyelids are quick clamps.

My back is my roof.
I am always at home.
I travel where my house walks.
It is a smooth stone.
It floats within the lake,
or rests in the dust.
My flesh lives tenderly
inside its bone.

MAY SWENSON

Earwig

The horny goloch is an awesome beast,
Supple and scaly;
lot It has two horns, and a hantle of feet,
And a forkie tailie.

TRADITIONAL SCOTTISH

Two Paddler's Songs

The Kayak Paddler's Joy at the Weather

When I'm out of the house in the open, I feel joy.
When I get out on the sea on haphazard, I feel joy.
If it is really fine weather, I feel joy.
If the sky really clears nicely, I feel joy.
May it continue thus for the good of my sealing!
May it continue thus for the good of my hunting!
May it continue thus for the good of my singing-match!
May it continue thus for the good of my drum-song!

Paddler's Song on Bad Hunting Weather

I got my poem in perfect order.
On the threshold of my tongue
Its arrangement was made.
But I failed, indeed, in my hunting.

TRADITIONAL Eskimo poems translated by William Thalbitzer

The Six Badgers

As I was a-hoeing, a-hoeing my lands
Six badgers came up with white wands in their hands.
They made a ring around me and, bowing, they said:
'Hurry home, Farmer George, for the table is spread!
There's pie in the oven, there's beef on the plate:
Hurry home, Farmer George, if you would not be late!'
So homeward I went, but could not understand
Why six fine dog-badgers with white wands in hand
Should seek me out hoeing and bow in a ring,
And all to inform me so common a thing!

ROBERT GRAVES

The Magical Mouse

I am the magical mouse
I don't eat cheese
I eat sunsets
And the tops of trees

I don't wear fur

I wear funnels
Of lost ships and the weather
That's under dead leaves
I am the magical mouse

I don't fear cats

Or woodowls
I do as I please
Always
I don't eat crusts
I am the magical mouse
I eat
Little birds and maidens

That taste like dust

KENNETH PATCHEN

Four Charms

A Charm for Hallowe'en

Hey-how for Hallowe'en!
All the witches to be seen,
Some black, and some green,
Hey-how for Hallowe'en!

A Charm for Sprains

Baldur and Woden went to the wood.
There was Baldur's foal's foot sprained.
Then charmed Woden, as well he knew how
For bone sprain, for blood sprain, for limb sprain.
Bone to bone, blood to blood, limb to limbs
As though they were glued.

A Charm

Nail three horseshoes to the foot of the
patient's bed, with a hammer laid crosswise upon them,
and then strike them, with the hammer held in the left
hand, saying:

Father, Son and Holy Ghost,
Nail the devil to the post.
Thrice I strike with holy crook,
One for God and one for Wod and one for Lok.

A Charm for Burns

Breathe three times on the burnt place and say:

Here come I to cure a burnt sore.
If the dead knew what the living endure,
The burnt sore would burn no more.

TRADITIONAL ENGLISH

Transmogrifications

To change into a hare, say this:

I shall go into a hare
much With sorrow and sighing and mickle care,
And I shall go in the Devil's name
Till I come home again.

To change back to a human shape, say this:

Hare, hare, God send thee care.
I am in a hare's likeness now
But I shall be in a woman's likeness even now.

TRADITIONAL ENGLISH

The Hairy Toe

Once there was a woman went out to pick beans,
and she found a Hairy Toe.
She took the Hairy Toe home with her,
and that night, when she went to bed,
the wind began to moan and groan.
Away off in the distance
she seemed to hear a voice crying,
'Who's got my Hair-r-ry To-o-oe?
Who's got my Hair-r-ry To-o-oe?'

The woman scrooched down,
'way down under the covers,
and about that time
the wind appeared to hit the house,
smoosh,
and the old house creaked and cracked
like something was trying to get in.
The voice had come nearer,
almost at the door now,
and it said,

'Where's my Hair-r-ry To-o-oe?
Who's got my Hair-r-ry To-o-oe?'

The woman scrooched further down
under the covers
and pulled them tight around her head.
The wind growled around the house
like some big animal
and r-r-um-mbled
over the chimbley.
All at once she heard the door cr-r-a-ack
and Something slipped in
and began to creep over the floor.
The floor went
cre-e-eak, cre-e-eak
at every step that thing took towards her bed.
The woman could almost feel
it bending over her bed.
Then in an awful voice it said:
'Where's my Hair-r-ry To-o-oe?
Who's got my Hair-r-ry To-o-oe?
You've got it!'

TRADITIONAL AMERICAN

The Knee

On earth there roams a lonely knee.
It's just a knee, that's all.
It's not a tent, it's not a tree,
it's just a knee, that's all.

In battle, long ago, a man
was riddled through and through.
The knee alone escaped unhurt
as if it were taboo.

Since then there roams a lonely knee,
it's just a knee, that's all.
It's not a tent, it's not a tree,
it's just a knee, that's all.

CHRISTIAN MORGENSTERN German poem translated by Max Knight

The Two Roots

A pair of pine roots, old and dark,
make conversation in the park.

The whispers where the top leaves grow
are echoed in the roots below.

An agèd squirrel sitting there
is knitting stockings for the pair.

The one says: squeak. The other: squawk.
That is enough for one day's talk.

CHRISTIAN MORGENSTERN German poem translated by Max Knight

Dunce Song

If I had a wife
I would love her as kings
Loved queens in the old days, or as princes
Maidens,
Met in the dew, by a stile, of a morning –
'How do you do, my pretty?'
And all of that.

If I had a wife
I would come home sometimes
Dressed like a stranger, and when she stared,
'Lady,'
I'd say, and woo her in wonder –
'How can there be such shining?'
And all of that.

If I had a wife
I would never be done
With remembering how it is now when, oh,
I am lonesome,
And no one is here but my dog and my cat –
'Well, old boys! Hungry?'
And all of that.

MARK VAN DOREN

The Thinker

My wife's new pink slippers
have gay pom-poms.
There is not a spot or a stain
on their satin toes or their sides.
All night they lie together
under her bed's edge.
Shivering I catch sight of them
and smile, in the morning.
Later I watch them
descending the stair,
hurrying through the doors
and round the table,
moving stiffly
with a shake of their gay pom-poms!
And I talk to them
in my secret mind
out of pure happiness.

WILLIAM CARLOS WILLIAMS

Meeting Mary

Hard by the Wildbrooks I met Mary,
When berries smelled sweet and hot.
Mary, I fancy, was seven years old,
And I am never mind what.

'What are you getting?' I asked Mary.
'Blackberries. What are you?'
'Toadflax,' I answered Mary, 'and mushrooms.'
'How many mushrooms?' 'Two.'

'Going to have blackberries stewed for dinner,
  Or blackberry jam?' said I.
'Not goin' to have neither,' said Mary;
'Goin' to have blackberry pie.'

'Aren't you lucky!' I said to Mary.
'And what sort of name have you got?'
'*My* name's Mary,' said Mary, 'what's *your* name?'
I told her never mind what.

'Good-bye, Mary.' 'Good-bye,' said Mary,
And went on picking and eating.
That's all about my meeting with Mary –
It's my favorite sort of meeting.

ELEANOR FARJEON

Teevee

In the house
of Mr. and Mrs. Spouse
he and she
would watch teevee
and never a word
between them spoken
until the day
the set was broken.

Then 'How do you do?'
said he to she,
'I don't believe
that we've met yet.
Spouse is my name.
What's yours?' he asked.

'Why, mine's the same!'
said she to he,
'Do you suppose that we could be –?'

But the set came suddenly right about,
and so they never did find out.

EVE MERRIAM

In the fall of '16

In the fall of '16 in the cool of the afternoon
I met Caroline under a white moon
There was an orchestra – Bingo-Bango
Playing for us to dance the tango
And the people all clapped as we arose
For her sweet face and my new clothes –

F. SCOTT FITZGERALD

Words

Words To Be Said on the Move

FLIT
FLUCTUATE
WOBBLE
WIGGLE
SHIVER
TIPTOE
PIROUETTE
TWIRL
TEETER

Odd Words

(to be spoken out loud, for fun)

HOBNOB
BARLEY
DOG-EARED
HOPSCOTCH
WINDWARD
OAF
EGG
OBOE
NUTMEG
OBLONG

Light Words
(to be said in windy or singing moods)

ARIEL
WILLOW
SPINNAKER
WHIRR
LISSOM
SIBILANT
PETTICOAT
NIMBLE
NIB

Heavy Words

(to be used in gloom or bad weather)

DUFFLE
BLUNDERBUSS
GALOSHES
BOWL
BEFUDDLED
MUGWUMP
PUMPKIN
CRUMB
BLOB

ALASTAIR REID

The Chair

A funny thing about a Chair:
You hardly ever think it's *there*.
To know a Chair is really it,
You sometimes have to go and sit.

THEODORE ROETHKE

The Ceiling

Suppose the Ceiling went Outside
And then caught Cold and Up and Died?
The only Thing we'd have for Proof
That he was Gone, would be the Roof;
I think it would be Most Revealing
To find out how the Ceiling's Feeling.

THEODORE ROETHKE

The Sniffle

A sniffle crouches on the terrace
to catch a victim he could harass.

And suddenly he jumps with vim
upon a man by name of Schrimm.

Paul Schrimm, responding with 'hatchoo',
is stuck with him the weekend through.

CHRISTIAN MORGENSTERN German poem translated by Max Knight

I never had a piece of toast

I never had a piece of toast
Particularly long and wide,
But fell upon the sanded floor
And always on the buttered side.

JAMES PAYN

The Indian of Peru, I think

The Indian of Peru, I think,
chewing
the leaf of a shrub
could run all day.
I, too,
with a few lines of verse, only two or three,
may be able
to see the day through.

CHARLES REZNIKOFF

Answers to Riddles

Riddles page 1

1 The letter R 2 Print on a page 3 The rising sun
4 A blood orange 5 A hen's egg

Who Said? page 2

The Lark

Acknowledgements

For permission to use copyright material acknowledgement is made to the following:

Poetry For 'Sitting Down, Looking Up' from *Northfield Poems* by A. R. Ammons to Cornell University Press; for 'The Tramp Tree' by Anthony Barton to the *Daily Mirror* Children's Literary Competition; for 'Sudden Shower' by Bashō from *An Introduction to Haiku* edited by Harold G. Henderson to Doubleday & Co. Inc.; for 'Eskimo Hunting Song' translated by Sir Maurice Bowra from *The Unwritten Song* edited by Willard R. Trask to the Macmillan Company of New York; for 'Nora' from *Bronzeville Boys and Girls* by Gwendolyn Brooks to Harper & Row Inc.; for 'Borrowed Armor' and 'The Whale' by Buson from *An Introduction to Haiku* edited by Harold G. Henderson to Doubleday & Co. Inc.; for 'Poem' by Susan David to the *Daily Mirror* Children's Literary Competition; for 'Dream Song' translated by D. Demetracopoulou from *The Unwritten Song* edited by Willard R. Trask to the Macmillan Company of New York; for 'The Rook' by James Earp to the *Daily Mirror* Children's Literary Competition; for 'Meeting Mary' from *Poems for Children* by Eleanor Farjeon to David Higham Associates Ltd and J. B. Lippincott Company; for 'In the fall of '16' from *Sleeping and Waking* by F. Scott Fitzgerald from Volume 3 of *The Bodley Head Scott Fitzgerald* to The Bodley Head and from *The Crack-Up* to New Directions Publishing Corporation; for 'The Ballad of Red Fox' by Melvin Walker la Follette from *The New Yorker, 1952* to the author; for 'The Six Badgers' from *The Penny Fiddle* by Robert Graves to the author and Collins-Knowlton-Wing Inc.; for 'Dull Day' by David Hill to the *Daily Mirror* Children's Literary Competition; for 'Gravel Paths' from *Catch Me a Wind* by Patricia Hubbell to Atheneum Publishers Inc.; for 'Tree-Disease' from *The Earth Owl and Other Moon People* by Ted Hughes to Faber & Faber Ltd; for 'The Bee' by Peter Kelso from *Once Around the Sun* to the Oxford University Press (Australia); for 'The Cock Again' by Kikaku from *An Introduction to Haiku* edited by Harold G. Henderson to Doubleday & Co. Inc.; for 'In a Sailplane' by James Kirkup to the author; for 'Storm Tide on Mejit' translated by Augustin Kramer and Willard R. Trask from *The Unwritten Song* edited by Willard R. Trask to the Macmillan Company of New York; for 'Roads' by Mei-Lan Law from *Once Around the Sun* to the Oxford University Press (Australia); for 'The Computer's Spring Greeting' by Gary Lewis to the author; for 'Over the Dark Highway' from *Cold Water* by Lou Lipsitz to Wesleyan University Press; for 'The Mouse that Gnawed the Oak-Tree down' from *Collected Poems* by Vachel Lindsay to the Macmillan Company of New York; for 'Which' by Walter de la Mare to the Literary Trustees of Walter de la Mare and the Society of Authors; for 'Mean Song' from *There is No Rhyme for Silver* by Eve Merriam to Atheneum Publishers Inc.; for 'Teevee' from *Catch a Little Rhyme* by Eve Merriam to the author and Atheneum Publishers Inc.; for 'The Knee', 'The Sniffle' and 'The Two Roots' from *Gallows Songs* by Christian Morgenstern translated by Max Knight to the University of California Press; for 'Social Studies' from *Woody and Me* by Mary Neville to Random House Inc.; for 'The Open-Air Bath' and 'The World Upside Down' by Onitsura from *An Introduction to Haiku* edited by Harold G. Henderson to Doubleday & Co. Inc.; for 'Day of Rabblement' from *When We Were Here Together* by Kenneth Patchen and for 'The Little Man with Wooden Hair' from *Hurrah for Anything*

List of Illustrations

Index of Titles and First Lines

Index of Poets, Translators and Collectors